A Satire on Intellectual Pretension

The Expert's Guide to Absolutely Wrong with Complete Confidence

A Serious Book for Very Important People Who Know Everything

Kalembwe Mwape

Table of Contents

Chapter 1: The Dunning-Kruger Mountain Resort: A Visitor's Guide 7
- How to Reach the Peak of Mount Stupid 8
- Why the View is Better When You Don't Know What You're Looking At 9
- Advanced Techniques for Avoiding Self-Awareness 11
- Field Exercises 13
- Conclusion 15

Chapter 2: The Social Media Philosopher's Stone 17
- Converting Random Thoughts into Universal Truths 17
- The Alchemist's Guide to Transmuting Thoughts into Wisdom 18
- The Art of Quote-Mining Without Context 20
- Why Reading Headlines Makes You an Expert 21
- Advanced Techniques: The Art of the Thread 23
- Practical Exercises 24
- Warning Signs You're Doing It Wrong 25
- Conclusion 26

Chapter 3: Name-Dropping for Beginners 28

A Satire on Intellectual Pretension

How to Reference Philosophers You've Never Read 28

How to Reference Nietzsche Without Reading Him 29

The Strategic Use of "Actually..." 31

When to Mention Your IQ Score in Casual Conversation 33

Advanced Name-Dropping Techniques 35

Emergency Protocols 36

Practical Exercises 38

Conclusion 39

Chapter 4: The Sophisticated Art of Being Wrong 40

Why Facts Are Just Opinions That Haven't Been Properly Challenged 40

Why Changing Your Mind is for the Weak 41

How to Double Down When Faced with Evidence 43

Advanced Cherry-Picking: A Fruit Picker's Guide to Arguments 45

Emergency Protocols for When You're Obviously Wrong 47

Practical Exercises in Wrongness 49

Conclusion: Embracing Your Inner Wrong 50

Chapter 5: Building Your Personal Brand of Insufferable 52

How to Ensure Everyone Knows You're the Smartest Person in Any Room 52

Crafting the Perfect Condescending Smile 52

The Art of Correcting People's Grammar Mid-Sentence 54

How to Turn Any Conversation into a Lecture 56

Personal Brand Elements 58

Monetization Strategies 60

Practical Exercises 61

Conclusion 63

Chapter 6: Networking with Other Experts 64

Finding Your Tribe of Fellow Know-It-Alls 64

How to Find People Who Are Also Always Right 64

Starting a Podcast When No One Asked 66

The LinkedIn Profile: Mastering the Humble Brag 68

Building Your Echo Chamber 70

Emergency Protocols for Network Threats 72

Chapter 1: The Dunning-Kruger Mountain Resort: A Visitor's Guide

en up, future thought leaders and proclaimed geniuses! You've made excellent decision to begin your ey to intellectual superiority, and e's no better place to start than our d-renowned Dunning-Kruger ntain Resort. Pack your bags (and e your self-awareness at home) — e about to embark on an ordinary adventure to the Peak of nt Stupid, where the air is thin and opinions are thick.

Practical Exercises 73
Conclusion 75

Chapter 7: The Etymology of Words You're Using Incorrectly 76

   How to Sound Smart by Mangling Ancient Languages 76

   Why Latin Makes You Sound Smarter 77

   Ancient Greek: The Ultimate Conversation Stopper 79

   Making Up Words That Sound Academic 80

   Etymological Warfare: Advanced Tactics 82

   Practical Exercises in Linguistic Confusion 84

   Emergency Protocols for Etymology Emergencies 85

   Conclusion 87

Chapter 8: Field Guide to Intellectual Superiority 88

   Identifying Lesser Minds in the Wild .. 88

   Identifying Lesser Minds in the Wild .. 89

   The Art of the Dismissive Hand Wave 91

   When to Say "Well, Actually..." 93

   Field Research Techniques 94

   Emergency Protocols for Intellectual Threats 96

- Practical Exercises in Superiority 98
- Conclusion 99

Appendix A: Common Phrases for the Modern Know-It-All.............................. 100
- Essential Vocabulary for the Professional Pseudo-Intellectual 100
- Section 1: "I don't mean to be pedantic, but..." (And Other Lies).................... 101
- Section 2: "As Someone Who..." 103
- Section 3: "In My Expert Opinion...". 104
- Section 4: Transitional Phrases for Intellectual Combat........................... 106
- Section 5: Power Phrases for Social Media 108
- Conclusion: The Power of Phrases.. 109

Appendix B: Certificates of Expertise .. 110
- Print-Your-Own Credentials and Other Intellectual Status Symbols 110
- Print-Your-Own Credentials 110
- How to Create a Wikipedia Page About Yourself 113
- Template for Your TED Talk Application 114
- Creating Your Academic-Looking Website 116
- Emergency Credential Defence Protocols 118

A Satire on Intellectual Pretension

How to Reach the Peak of Mount Stupid

Let's get one thing straight: reaching the summit of Mount Stupid isn't for the faint of heart or the cursed with humility. The first rule of ascending to intellectual greatness is to immediately discard any notion that expertise requires actual study, experience, or – God forbid – nuanced understanding. Those are for the weak-minded masses who waste years "learning" and "practicing" their craft.

The true path to the peak is much more efficient. Simply read one (1) article about any complex topic, preferably from a questionable source on social media, and immediately begin correcting others who have spent decades in the field. Remember: confidence is directly proportional to ignorance. The less you know, the more certain you should be.

Pro tip: If someone challenges your expertise, simply respond with "Well, actually..." and reference that one YouTube video you watched at 2 AM. Nothing screams "intellectual heavyweight" like explaining quantum physics to a physics professor based on your understanding of "Quantum Physics Explained in 10 Minutes (For Dummies)."

Why the View is Better When You Don't Know What You're Looking At

Here's the beautiful thing about reaching the Peak of Mount Stupid: everything becomes crystal clear when you don't understand any of the complexities. It's like wearing glasses

Practical Exercises 73
Conclusion 75
Chapter 7: The Etymology of Words You're Using Incorrectly 76
How to Sound Smart by Mangling Ancient Languages 76
Why Latin Makes You Sound Smarter 77
Ancient Greek: The Ultimate Conversation Stopper 79
Making Up Words That Sound Academic 80
Etymological Warfare: Advanced Tactics 82
Practical Exercises in Linguistic Confusion 84
Emergency Protocols for Etymology Emergencies 85
Conclusion 87
Chapter 8: Field Guide to Intellectual Superiority 88
Identifying Lesser Minds in the Wild .. 88
Identifying Lesser Minds in the Wild .. 89
The Art of the Dismissive Hand Wave 91
When to Say "Well, Actually..." 93
Field Research Techniques 94
Emergency Protocols for Intellectual Threats 96

Practical Exercises in Superiority 98

Conclusion 99

Appendix A: Common Phrases for the Modern Know-It-All 100

Essential Vocabulary for the Professional Pseudo-Intellectual 100

Section 1: "I don't mean to be pedantic, but..." (And Other Lies) 101

Section 2: "As Someone Who..." 103

Section 3: "In My Expert Opinion...". 104

Section 4: Transitional Phrases for Intellectual Combat 106

Section 5: Power Phrases for Social Media 108

Conclusion: The Power of Phrases.. 109

Appendix B: Certificates of Expertise .. 110

Print-Your-Own Credentials and Other Intellectual Status Symbols 110

Print-Your-Own Credentials 110

How to Create a Wikipedia Page About Yourself 113

Template for Your TED Talk Application 114

Creating Your Academic-Looking Website 116

Emergency Credential Defence Protocols 118

Conclusion: The Art of Credential Creation 120
Index of Obscure References to Drop in Conversation 121
  (Arranged by pretentiousness level) 121
  Emergency Backup References 124
  Situational Applications 125
Copyright 127

Chapter 1: The Dunning-Kruger Mountain Resort: A Visitor's Guide

Listen up, future thought leaders and self-proclaimed geniuses! You've made the excellent decision to begin your journey to intellectual superiority, and there's no better place to start than our world-renowned Dunning-Kruger Mountain Resort. Pack your bags (and leave your self-awareness at home) – we're about to embark on an extraordinary adventure to the Peak of Mount Stupid, where the air is thin and the opinions are thick.

that filter out all that messy nuance and context that keeps getting in the way of your bold, sweeping declarations about how the world works.

From this vantage point, you'll discover that every complex social issue actually has a simple solution that experts are just too stupid to see. Economics? Just print more money. Climate change? Just move to Mars. Mental health? Just be happy! See how easy problem-solving becomes when you're unburdened by knowledge?

The view from the peak allows you to see everything in beautiful black and white, free from those annoying shades of grey that plague actual experts. Remember: if someone suggests that an issue is complex, they're probably just not as smart as you are.

Advanced Techniques for Avoiding Self-Awareness

Now, maintaining your position at the peak requires constant vigilance against the greatest threat to your intellectual superiority: self-awareness. Here are some battle-tested techniques to keep that pesky reflective thinking at bay:

The Echo Chamber Workout

- Immediately unfriend anyone who disagrees with you
- Join online communities that validate your existing beliefs
- Label all contrary evidence as "fake news"
- Bonus points if you create a podcast where you only interview people who think exactly like you do

A Satire on Intellectual Pretension

The Cognitive Dissonance Defence Shield

When confronted with evidence that contradicts your beliefs, deploy these proven countermeasures:

1. Attack the source ("Oh, you got that from a peer-reviewed journal? How mainstream.")
2. Move the goalposts ("That's not what I meant, what I actually meant was...")
3. Appeal to conspiracy ("That's just what they want you to think!")
4. When all else fails, type "DO YOUR RESEARCH" in all caps and leave the conversation

The Superiority Maintenance Routine

Start each day by:

- Reading your own social media posts from yesterday

- Admiring your collection of out-of-context quotes
- Practicing your condescending smile in the mirror
- Writing a LinkedIn post about how you're disrupting an industry you know nothing about

Remember, the key to maintaining your position at the Peak of Mount Stupid is to never, ever climb down into the Valley of Understanding. Once you start actually learning about a subject, you might develop that most dangerous of traits: intellectual humility. And we can't have that, can we?

Field Exercises

To cement your position as a peak performer, complete the following exercises:

A Satire on Intellectual Pretension

1. Find a complex academic paper. Read only the abstract, then write a 1,000-word critique explaining why the authors are wrong.

2. Attend a lecture in a field you know nothing about. Raise your hand at least three times to begin questions with "Actually..."

3. Start a Twitter thread explaining why experts in a field are all wrong, based solely on your gut feelings.

4. Bonus Challenge: Explain blockchain to your grandmother after watching exactly one TikTok about cryptocurrency.

Conclusion

Congratulations! By now, you should be well-equipped to reach and maintain your position at the Peak of Mount Stupid. Remember: the key to being an expert is not years of study and practical experience – it's the unshakeable conviction that you already know everything worth knowing.

In our next chapter, we'll explore how to leverage your newfound position to become a thought leader on social media, where the depth of your insights should never exceed the character limit of a tweet.

Remember: If you're starting to doubt yourself, you're doing it wrong. True expertise is never having to say "I don't know" or "I might be wrong." Now go forth and spread your wisdom to the unwashed masses who foolishly believe in things like "peer review" and "empirical evidence."

Chapter 2: The Social Media Philosopher's Stone

Converting Random Thoughts into Universal Truths

Ah, welcome back, aspiring sage of the digital age! Now that you've mastered the art of baseless confidence at the Dunning-Kruger Mountain Resort, it's time to transform your shower thoughts into profound universal wisdom. After all, why spend years studying philosophy when you can just post deep-sounding quotes over sunset backgrounds?

A Satire on Intellectual Pretension

The Alchemist's Guide to Transmuting Thoughts into Wisdom

Let's begin with a fundamental truth of the modern age: the shorter the thought, the deeper it must be. Twitter isn't just a social media platform — it's the modern equivalent of Plato's Academy, except instead of lengthy dialogues, we have hot takes and hashtags. And you, dear reader, are about to become its next great philosopher.

The Basic Elements of Social Media Philosophy

1. The Profound Format
- Start every post with "Nobody talks about..."
- Follow with something everybody talks about

- End with "Let that sink in" or "Read that again"

Example: *"Nobody talks about how we're all just living on a spinning rock in space. Let that sink in. #DeepThoughts #WakeUp"*

2. The Authority Formula
- Begin statements with "Science shows..." or "Studies prove..."
- Never cite these studies
- If challenged, respond with "Do your own research"
- Bonus points for using "Quantum" in completely irrelevant contexts

3. The Engagement Algorithm
- Post obvious observations as ground-breaking insights
- Example: *"Water is just boneless ice. Think about that."*
- When someone points out it's nonsense, reply "That's exactly what they want you to think"

A Satire on Intellectual Pretension

The Art of Quote-Mining Without Context

Remember: context is for cowards. Real social media philosophers know that any quote can mean anything if you try hard enough. Here's your guide to professional quote-mining:

Step 1: Finding Quotes
- Google "inspirational quotes"
- Pick something that sounds vaguely profound
- Attribute it to someone more famous than the actual author
- Morgan Freeman and Einstein are always safe bets

Step 2: Recontextualization
- Take scientific terms out of context

- Apply quantum physics to your dating life
- Use "paradigm shift" at least once per post
- Throw in "synergy" for good measure

Step 3: Application

WRONG: *"Einstein was discussing relative motion in physics."*

RIGHT: *"Einstein's theory of relativity clearly proves that all truth is relative, especially on dating apps."*

Why Reading Headlines Makes You an Expert

Listen closely, because this is where true mastery begins. Reading entire articles is for amateurs. Real experts form unshakeable opinions based solely on headlines. Here's why:

A Satire on Intellectual Pretension

The Benefits of Headline-Only Expertise:

1. Time Efficiency
- Why waste 10 minutes reading when you can spend 2 hours arguing in the comments?
- More time to share your opinions means more people enlightened
- Reading the article might confuse you with facts

2. Opinion Purity
- Facts only muddy the waters of pure speculation
- Your gut feeling is more reliable than peer-reviewed research
- If someone posts a link disproving your point, simply respond "Fake news"

3. Engagement Optimization
- The wronger you are, the more comments you'll get
- Being corrected just means you're disrupting the status quo
- Every angry reaction is proof you're "making people think"

Advanced Techniques: The Art of the Thread

Now that you've mastered basic social media philosophy, it's time to advance to thread-making. A thread is your chance to turn a simple thought into a 47-part manifesto about society, consciousness, or why your coffee order reveals deep truths about capitalism.

The Thread Formula:
1. Start with "📜 THREAD (1/47)"

2. Make each point more outlandish than the last
3. Connect completely unrelated concepts
4. End with a link to your newsletter

Example:

📜 *THREAD: Why your morning coffee proves we're living in a simulation (1/47)*

Have you ever noticed how coffee is brown? So are trees. Coincidence? Let me explain how this proves consciousness is a collective hallucination... (2/47)

Practical Exercises

1. Take any common phrase and explain why it's actually problematic:

"Good morning" → Why do we assume mornings are good? A thread on temporal prejudice...

2. Find a complex scientific concept and apply it to dating:

"Schrödinger's Text: If you haven't checked your messages, you're both ghosted and not ghosted."

3. Create a profound observation:
- Look at any ordinary object
- Squint really hard
- Write whatever random connection comes to mind
- Add "Society isn't ready for this conversation"

Warning Signs You're Doing It Wrong

- You fact-check before posting
- You consider other perspectives

- You admit when you're wrong
- You read entire articles
- You use credible sources

If you catch yourself doing any of these, immediately post a quote about how education kills creativity, preferably misattributed to Einstein or Buddha.

Conclusion

Remember, dear student, social media philosophy isn't about being right – it's about being confident and getting those sweet, sweet engagement metrics. The truth is whatever gets the most retweets, and wisdom is measured in followers, not understanding.

In our next chapter, we'll explore the art of name-dropping philosophers you've never read but saw quoted on Instagram. Until then, keep posting, keep pontificating, and remember: the less you know about something, the more qualified you are to explain it to others.

Chapter 3: Name-Dropping for Beginners

How to Reference Philosophers You've Never Read

Welcome back, budding intellectual! Now that you've mastered the art of social media philosophy, it's time to add some gravitas to your profound observations. Nothing says "I'm a serious thinker" quite like casually dropping the names of philosophers you've never read into everyday conversations. Let's dive into the art of philosophical name-dropping, or as Wittgenstein would say... well, actually, let's not get into what he would say. That's exactly the kind of detail that might expose our carefully crafted façade.

How to Reference Nietzsche Without Reading Him

First things first: Nietzsche is your new best friend. Why? Because he's perfectly misunderstood, widely misquoted, and absolutely perfect for your purposes. Here's your comprehensive guide to speaking about Nietzsche without ever opening "Thus Spoke Zarathustra" (which, by the way, you should claim is "problematic" without elaborating).

Essential Nietzsche-Dropping Techniques:

1. The Basic Package
- Mention "God is dead" at least once per conversation
- Never provide context

A Satire on Intellectual Pretension

- Look disappointed when others don't understand the "deeper meaning"
- Bonus: Sigh heavily and say "It's a metaphor" when challenged

2. Advanced Applications

- Apply "Will to Power" to literally anything
- Example: *"This coffee shop's pricing strategy clearly demonstrates Nietzsche's Will to Power"*
- If someone actually knows Nietzsche, quickly pivot to Sartre

3. Emergency Responses

When cornered about actual Nietzsche philosophy:

- "That's a common misinterpretation"
- "Have you read it in the original German?"

- "I prefer his earlier, more obscure works"
- "That's exactly what his sister wanted you to think"

The Strategic Use of "Actually..."

Ah, "Actually..." – the intellectual poseur's secret weapon. This simple word, when deployed correctly, can transform any conversation into an opportunity to showcase your superior knowledge, regardless of whether you possess any.

The "Actually" Technique:

1. Basic Deployment
- Wait for someone to make any statement

- Begin your response with "Actually..."
- Contradict them with something you read in a tweet
- Look smug

2. Advanced Applications

Regular Person: *"The sky is blue today."*

You: *"Actually, what we perceive as blue is just a social construct influenced by linguistic relativism, as Wittgenstein might argue... if he were alive to see how Instagram filters have revolutionized our chromatic paradigm."*

3. Master Level Moves

- Correct people's grammar mid-sentence
- Point out etymological "facts" you just made up
- Use "epistemologically speaking" in casual conversation

- Mention how things are done "in Europe" (be vague about which part)

When to Mention Your IQ Score in Casual Conversation

The art of IQ score mention requires the delicacy of a sledgehammer and the timing of a broken clock. Here's your guide to working your allegedly high IQ into any conversation, especially when it's completely irrelevant.

Perfect Moments to Mention Your IQ:

1. During Simple Tasks
- While struggling to open a jar
- After spelling something wrong

- When getting lost despite using GPS

Example: *"It's funny how my 157 IQ doesn't help with parallel parking!"*

2. In Intellectual Discussions
- When losing an argument
- When someone uses facts you can't refute
- When you don't understand something

Example: *"Well, with my IQ of 157, I can see why you might think that..."*

3. Completely Random Situations
- Ordering coffee
- Checking the weather
- Tying your shoes

Example: *"As someone with a high IQ, I find these shoelace designs rather pedestrian"*

Advanced Name-Dropping Techniques

Now that you've mastered the basics, let's explore some advanced techniques for appearing intellectual in any situation.

The Philosopher's Toolkit:

1. The Obscure Reference
- Never mention popular philosophers
- The more unpronounceable the name, the better
- Make up philosophers if necessary — who's going to check?

2. The Cross-Cultural Gambit
- Reference Eastern philosophy vaguely

A Satire on Intellectual Pretension

- Say "As the ancient mystics knew..."
- Never specify which mystics
- If pressed, mumble something about "ancient wisdom"

3. The Academic Special
- Start sentences with "In the academy..."
- Never specify which academy
- Use "problematize" instead of "question"
- Say "It's more nuanced than that" without explaining how

Emergency Protocols

Sometimes you'll encounter actual experts. Don't panic! Here's your emergency response kit:

When Someone Actually Knows the Subject:

1. The Tactical Retreat
- "I'm approaching this from a different paradigm"
- "We'll have to agree to disagree"
- "That's just your Western logical framework talking"
- "I'm more interested in the meta-conversation"

2. The Counter-Attack
- Question their credentials
- Mention your blog
- Reference a podcast they haven't heard of
- Say "That's exactly what the mainstream wants you to think"

Practical Exercises

1. The Coffee Shop Challenge

Turn your local coffee shop into a philosophical symposium:

- Order a simple coffee using at least three philosopher references
- Explain why your drink choice reflects existential dread
- Look disappointed when the barista doesn't want to discuss Hegel

2. The Social Media Experiment

- Post a picture of your bookshelf
- Make sure Kafka is visible (unread, of course)
- Caption it with "Light weekend reading Intellectual Life"
- Bonus points for a strategically placed copy of "Being and Nothingness"

Conclusion

Remember, true intellectual posturing isn't about actually knowing things – it's about making others feel bad for not knowing the things you're pretending to know. In our next chapter, we'll explore the sophisticated art of being wrong with unshakeable confidence.

Until then, keep practicing your condescending smile and remember: if someone calls you out on your pseudo-intellectual behaviour, just quote Derrida out of context. No one knows what he meant anyway.

A Satire on Intellectual Pretension

Chapter 4: The Sophisticated Art of Being Wrong

Why Facts Are Just Opinions That Haven't Been Properly Challenged

Welcome back, champions of certainty! In our previous chapters, we've covered how to appear knowledgeable without the burden of actual knowledge. Now, we'll tackle the most crucial skill in your intellectual arsenal: being wrong with unshakeable confidence. After all, what's the point of having opinions if you're going to let little things like "evidence" or "facts" change them?

Why Changing Your Mind is for the Weak

First, let's establish our fundamental principle: consistency is far more important than accuracy. Think about it – would you rather be right, or would you rather maintain your reputation as someone who has never admitted to being wrong about anything? The answer is obvious to any true intellectual warrior.

The Foundations of Steadfast Wrongness:

1. The Immovable Mind Technique
- Treat your first impression as eternal truth
- Consider all new information as a personal attack

- Remember: learning is just admitting you didn't know everything
- Bonus points for saying "I've always believed this" about opinions you formed yesterday

2. The Defensive Arsenal

When presented with contrary evidence:

- *"That's just your perspective"*
- *"I reject your reality and substitute my own"*
- *"Facts are tools of the establishment"*
- *"Have you considered that all knowledge is subjective?"*

3. Advanced Techniques

- Claim that being proven wrong just strengthens your original point
- Insist that evidence supporting your position exists but is being suppressed

- Declare that you're operating on a "different level of understanding"
- When all else fails, claim to be playing devil's advocate

How to Double Down When Faced with Evidence

Now we enter the grand arena of doubling down – the black belt level of being wrong. When confronted with irrefutable evidence that contradicts your position, you must not merely maintain your stance; you must escalate it to previously unimagined heights of wrongness.

The Double-Down Protocol:

1. Initial Response
- Question the validity of the evidence

- Attack the credibility of the source
- Claim the evidence actually supports your position
- Insist that "new research" (which you can't cite) proves you right

2. Secondary Defence
- Move the goalposts so far they're in another stadium
- Change the subject while pretending you haven't
- Introduce completely irrelevant historical facts
- Start every sentence with "Well, technically..."

3. Nuclear Options
- Declare that you're being persecuted for your ideas
- Claim to have secret information you can't reveal
- Insist that you're actually conducting a social experiment
- Quote George Orwell out of context

Advanced Cherry-Picking: A Fruit Picker's Guide to Arguments

Cherry-picking is an art form, and you're about to become Michelangelo. The key is to treat evidence like a buffet – take what supports your position and pretend the rest doesn't exist.

Master Class in Selective Evidence:

1. The Basic Harvest
- Find one study that supports your view
- Ignore the hundreds that don't
- Claim consensus based on your single source
- If challenged, say "Research is ongoing"

A Satire on Intellectual Pretension

2. Statistical Sleight of Hand

- Use percentages when they sound impressive
- Switch to raw numbers when they don't
- Make graphs with manipulated axes
- If caught, claim you're "challenging traditional statistical paradigms"

3. The Context Elimination Chamber

- Remove all nuance from complex issues
- Present correlation as causation
- Use anecdotes as universal proof
- Respond to criticism with "You're oversimplifying a complex issue"

Emergency Protocols for When You're Obviously Wrong

Sometimes, despite your best efforts, you'll find yourself in a situation where your wrongness is so apparent that even your usual techniques won't work. Fear not! We have protocols for these dire situations.

The WRONG Protocol (Wrongness Response & Outrage Generation):

1. Widen the Scope
- Make the argument so broad it becomes meaningless
- "We're actually discussing the nature of truth itself"

A Satire on Intellectual Pretension

2. Reframe the Debate
- Claim you were actually making a different point all along
- "This just proves my meta-argument about discourse"

3. Obfuscate with Complexity
- Introduce unnecessary philosophical concepts
- Use academic jargon incorrectly but confidently

4. Negative Attribution
- Question the motives of those proving you wrong
- "Only a shill would have access to this many facts"

5. Grandstand and Exit
- Declare the discussion beneath you
- Leave dramatically while citing your busy schedule

Practical Exercises in Wrongness

1. The Wikipedia Challenge
- Find a Wikipedia article about something you know nothing about
- Argue with the cited experts in the talk page
- Insist your personal blog is a more reliable source

2. The Conference Call Gambit
- Make a completely incorrect statement about your field of expertise
- When corrected, say "That's exactly what I meant"
- Repeat your wrong statement with more confidence

3. The Social Media Spiral
- Post an obviously incorrect fact
- Respond to each correction with an even more incorrect statement
- End by claiming you've "won" the debate

Conclusion: Embracing Your Inner Wrong

Remember, dear student, being wrong isn't a state of mind – it's a lifestyle. With these techniques, you can maintain any position, no matter how incorrect, in the face of overwhelming evidence to the contrary. The key is to never, ever admit uncertainty about anything.

In our next chapter, we'll explore how to turn your unwavering wrongness into a personal brand, complete with merchandising opportunities and a

Patreon account. Until then, stay wrong and stay strong!

A Satire on Intellectual Pretension

Chapter 5: Building Your Personal Brand of Insufferable

How to Ensure Everyone Knows You're the Smartest Person in Any Room

Welcome back, aspiring thought leaders! Now that you've mastered the art of being confidently wrong, it's time to monetize your intellectual superiority. In today's personal brand marketplace, being insufferable isn't just a personality trait – it's a business model.

Crafting the Perfect Condescending Smile

Before we dive into brand building, we must perfect your physical presentation. The condescending smile is your logo, your trademark, your visual mission statement. It needs to say, "I'm not just judging you; I'm cataloguing your intellectual failures for my upcoming TEDx talk."

The Anatomy of Condescension:

1. The Basic Form
- Raise left eyebrow exactly 3.7 millimeters
- Curl right side of mouth upward at 23-degree angle
- Tilt head slightly, suggesting you're examining a curious specimen
- Maintain eye contact that says *"I'm not looking at you, I'm looking through you"*

2. Advanced Techniques
- The "Oh, You Still Believe In Facts?" head tilt

- The "I Read This In The Original Sanskrit" nose wrinkle
- The "Actually, Time Is A Social Construct" eye roll
- The "I'm Not Sighing At You, I'm Sighing At Society" exhale

3. Environmental Modifications
- Always position yourself near bookshelves
- Carry a worn copy of "Being and Nothingness" (never open it)
- Have a coffee cup with a quote from your own blog
- Wear glasses without prescription lenses

The Art of Correcting People's Grammar Mid-Sentence

Nothing says "I'm intellectually superior" quite like interrupting someone's heartfelt story about their grandmother's passing to correct their usage of "who" versus "whom." This is your moment to shine!

Grammar Correction Hierarchy:

1. Beginner Level
- Correct "their" vs. "they're"
- Point out split infinitives
- Mention Oxford commas unprompted
- Say "irregardless isn't a word" (ignore dictionary updates)

2. Intermediate Techniques

Speaker: *"I'm really excited about—"*

You: *"You mean you're really 'enthused.' 'Excited' implies a physiological state of arousal."*

Speaker: *"My dog just died—"*

You: *"Actually, it's 'My dog has just died.' Present perfect tense indicates a recent past action with present consequences."*

3. Advanced Manoeuvres
- Correct people speaking their native language when you've only studied it for two weeks
- Introduce obscure grammatical terms from dead languages
- Explain why emoji are destroying civilization
- Begin sentences with "In proper English..."

How to Turn Any Conversation into a Lecture

The key to personal brand building is visibility. Every conversation is an opportunity to demonstrate your vast knowledge of subjects you just googled.

Conversation Hijacking Strategies:

1. The Topic Transition Protocol
- Wait for any pause
- Say "This reminds me of an interesting fact..."
- Launch into a 45-minute monologue
- Ignore all attempts to resume original conversation

2. The Expert Insertion Method
Friend: *"I love this pizza!"*

You: *"Actually, the concept of pizza as we know it emerged during the socioeconomic upheavals of 16th century Naples. This reminds me of my doctoral thesis on the ontological implications of fast food in late-stage capitalism..."*

3. *The Intellectual Ambush*
- Memorize random facts about everything
- Practice linking any topic to your favourite philosophical theory
- Develop catchphrases like "Well, as a student of critical theory..."
- Always have a relevant quote that you definitely didn't just make up

Personal Brand Elements

Now let's build your insufferable personal brand piece by piece.

Essential Brand Components:
1. *Social Media Presence*
- Profile picture: Black and white, looking pensively off-camera

- Bio: Include "polymath," "renaissance soul," and "professional contrarian"
- Header image: Your own quote overlaid on a sunset
- Pinned tweet: Something cryptic about consciousness

2. Content Strategy

- Monday: Post about how labels limit intellectual discourse
- Tuesday: Share a thread about why everyone else is wrong
- Wednesday: Critique popular culture using obscure philosophy
- Thursday: Explain why your morning coffee reflects the universe's entropy
- Friday: Start intellectual fights in random comment sections
- Weekend: Retweet yourself

3. Visual Branding
- Wardrobe: All black, suggesting deep thoughts
- Accessories: Unnecessary glasses, weathered notebook
- Props: Stacked books in every photo
- Expression: Permanent look of mild disappointment

Monetization Strategies

Because true intellectuals understand that wisdom has a price tag.

Revenue Streams:

1. The Basic Package
- Start a Substack newsletter: "Thoughts That Are Too Deep for Twitter"

- Create online courses: "Introduction to Being Insufferable"
- Write an eBook: "Why I'm Right and You're Not: A Memoir"
- Launch a podcast: "Actually: Conversations with Myself"

2. Advanced Income Generation
- Offer consulting services on how to be more pretentious
- Create merchandise with your most condescending quotes
- Host workshops on advanced name-dropping techniques
- Sell NFTs of your most controversial tweets

Practical Exercises

1. The Coffee Shop Challenge
- Order a simple drink in the most complicated way possible

- Explain the philosophical implications of your order to everyone in line
- Write a LinkedIn post about the experience
- Title it "What My Barista Taught Me About Quantum Physics"

2. The Networking Event Takeover
- Attend any professional gathering
- Redirect every conversation to your theory about consciousness
- Collect business cards while looking unimpressed
- Follow up with links to your podcast

3. The Social Media Ascension
- Post a thread about why threads are destroying discourse
- While posting a thread
- About the irony of posting threads
- Meta-commentary is key

Conclusion

Remember, building your brand of insufferable isn't just about being unbearable – it's about being unbearable at scale. Your goal is to ensure that when people think of pretentious pseudo-intellectuals, they think of you first.

Chapter 6: Networking with Other Experts

Finding Your Tribe of Fellow Know-It-Alls

Welcome back, intellectual maverick! Now that you've established your personal brand of insufferable, it's time to build your network of equally self-assured individuals. Remember: even a lone genius needs an audience of other self-proclaimed geniuses to validate their unearned confidence.

How to Find People Who Are Also Always Right

The first step in building your intellectual echo chamber is identifying suitable peers – those rare individuals who, like you, have achieved perfect knowledge of all subjects through the power of pure assumption.

Identifying Your Peers:

1. Key Indicators of Fellow Experts
- They correct strangers' grammar on social media
- Their profile includes "autodidact" or "polymath"
- They've started at least three sentences with "Well, actually" in the past hour
- They reference Kafka without having read him
- They have strong opinions about fonts

2. Natural Habitats
Prime locations for expert-spotting:

- *University coffee shops (never actually enter the university)*
- *Independent bookstore philosophy sections*
- *Twitter threads about consciousness*
- *TED Talk comment sections*

3. Recognition Signals
- Carry a visible copy of "Thus Spoke Zarathustra"
- Wear a turtleneck in summer
- Make audible "hmmm" sounds when others speak
- Take notes with a fountain pen for no reason
- Randomly mention your IQ score

Starting a Podcast When No One Asked

In today's intellectual landscape, having a podcast isn't just an option –

it's a declaration of your unwarranted sense of authority. Here's how to create the perfect echo chamber for your thoughts.

Podcast Essential Elements:

1. The Perfect Title
- "The [Your Name] Experience"
- "Thoughts from the Intellectual Dark Web Adjacent"
- "Actually: A Journey into Truth"
- "Beyond Knowledge: Transcending Facts with [Your Name]"
- "The Meta-Cognitive Revolution"

2. Episode Formats
- Monologues about simple concepts you've overcomplicated
- Interviews with other podcasters who will interview you back
- Live readings of your viral tweets

- "Deconstructing" popular media no one asked you to analyse
- Special episodes where you explain why other podcasts are wrong

3. Technical Requirements
- Expensive microphone (visible in all social media photos)
- Acoustic panels (primarily for aesthetic)
- Intro music that sounds vaguely intellectual
- Sound effects for when you make particularly profound points
- A co-host who never disagrees with you

The LinkedIn Profile: Mastering the Humble Brag

LinkedIn is your stage for professional-grade intellectual peacocking. Here's how to optimize your profile for maximum self-importance.

LinkedIn Optimization Strategy:

1. The Perfect Header
- "Thought Leader | Paradigm Shifter | Professional Devil's Advocate"
- "Intellectual Explorer | Knowledge Synthesizer | Coffee Enthusiast"
- "Questioning Everything | Answering Nothing | Available for Speaking Engagements"

2. Experience Section

Current Role: *Chief Philosophical Officer at Self-Employed*

Previous: *Head of Cognitive Disruption at My Own Thoughts*

Education: *University of Life, School of Hard Knocks, YouTube University*

3. Activity Feed
- Share articles without reading them
- Write "Agree?" on other people's posts
- Post long stories about how you enlightened your Uber driver
- Begin every post with "Unpopular opinion:"

Building Your Echo Chamber

A true intellectual leader needs a carefully curated group of yes-people who will never challenge their assumptions.

Echo Chamber Construction Guide:

1. Member Selection Criteria
- Must agree with everything you say

- Should have similar unearned confidence
- Required to retweet all your threads
- Must attend your virtual seminars
- Should reference you as a primary source

2. Maintenance Protocols
- Regular validation sessions disguised as "masterminds"
- Group chat for sharing screenshots of your critics
- Weekly book club (discussing books none of you have read)
- Monthly "thought leadership" summits in expensive coffee shops

3. Growth Strategies
- Create a "selective" community with no actual selection criteria
- Charge high prices for "exclusive" access to your thoughts

- Start an "intellectual movement" based on your morning shower thoughts
- Launch a certification program in your made-up methodology

Emergency Protocols for Network Threats

Sometimes your network may be infiltrated by actual experts. Here's how to handle these threats to your intellectual ecosystem.

Threat Response Procedures:

1. The Expert Infiltration
- Question their credentials while citing none of your own
- Claim they're too "mainstream" to understand your insights

- Declare their field of expertise obsolete
- Start a rumour about paradigm shifts making their knowledge irrelevant

2. The Fact Checker

- Insist that fact-checking is a tool of the establishment
- Claim you're operating on a "different epistemological framework"
- Declare that truth is relative (only when you're wrong)
- Start a thread about why being right is actually wrong

Practical Exercises

1. The Conference Creation

- Organize a conference about "The Future of Thought"

A Satire on Intellectual Pretension

- Ensure all speakers are equally unqualified
- Charge excessive prices for "VIP networking"
- End every session with "We'll continue this discussion in my course"

2. The Mastermind Group Launch
- Create an application process that accepts everyone
- Name it something pretentious like "The Paradigm Collective"
- Require members to quote you regularly
- Establish secret handshakes and terminology

3. The Community Building Challenge
- Start a Discord server for "high-level thinkers"
- Create arbitrary ranks based on agreement with you

- Institute daily validation ceremonies
- Ban anyone who brings up peer-reviewed research

Conclusion

Remember, networking isn't about making genuine connections – it's about building a fortress of mutual delusion strong enough to withstand any assault by actual experts. Your network should be an impenetrable bubble of shared certainty, where facts are optional and confidence is mandatory.

A Satire on Intellectual Pretension

Chapter 7: The Etymology of Words You're Using Incorrectly

How to Sound Smart by Mangling Ancient Languages

Welcome back, linguistic revolutionaries! Now that you've built your network of fellow pseudo-intellectuals, it's time to develop your most powerful weapon: the ability to confidently misuse words while claiming deep historical knowledge of their origins. Remember, it's not about being right — it's about being so confidently wrong that others question their own understanding.

Why Latin Makes You Sound Smarter

Let's begin with the cornerstone of intellectual posturing: dropping Latin phrases into everyday conversation. Nothing says "I'm educated" quite like misusing a dead language.

Essential Latin Mangling Techniques:

1. Basic Latin Deployment
- Use "per se" in every sentence, per se
- Pronounce "etc." as "et cetera" with excessive emphasis
- End arguments with "QED" regardless of context
- Add "ad hoc" to random phrases
- Declare "ipso facto" after any statement, related or not

2. Advanced Latin Misuse

Ordering coffee: *"I would like, vis-à-vis your finest brew, a grande latte, in medias res, with extra foam, ad infinitum."*

Work email: *"Per my previous email, viz. the TPS reports, we need to establish a quid pro quo paradigm shift, ex post facto."*

3. Emergency Latin Protocols

When caught using Latin incorrectly:

- Claim you're using the "rare" or "archaic" meaning
- Insist you're quoting "pre-classical" usage
- Declare that pronunciation is a social construct
- Switch to Greek immediately

Ancient Greek: The Ultimate Conversation Stopper

Why use simple English words when you can mispronounce Greek ones? Remember: the more obscure the reference, the less likely anyone can correct you.

Greek Word Arsenal:

1. Basic Greek Flexing
- Pronounce "paradigm" differently each time
- Use "epistemological" for any knowledge-related concept
- Throw "ontological" into discussions about coffee
- Add "meta-" to random words

2. Advanced Greek Deployment
- Claim everything is a "dialectic"

A Satire on Intellectual Pretension

- Use "hermeneutic" as both noun and verb
- Insist on saying "praxis" instead of "practice"
- Reference the "logos" of mundane objects

3. Expert-Level Greek Abuse

At a restaurant: *"The epistemological framework of this menu's ontological structure creates a dialectical relationship with my phenomenological experience of hunger."*

Translation: *"I can't decide what to order."*

Making Up Words That Sound Academic

When existing words aren't pretentious enough, it's time to create your own.

The key is to make them sound just plausible enough that people are afraid to admit they don't know them.

Word Creation Guidelines:

1. Basic Word Formation
- Add "-ization" to anything
- Combine random Greek and Latin roots
- Insert "post-" before existing concepts
- Create new "-isms"

2. Sample Invented Terms
- "Metamorphosynthesis" (n): The process of changing while staying the same
- "Cognito-temporal displacement" (n): Being late to meetings
- "Trans-caffeinated dialectics" (n): Coffee shop philosophy

- "Post-ironic pre-modernism" (n): Whatever you want it to mean

3. Usage Examples

"Through the lens of proto-metaphysical cognito-synthesis, we can observe the inherent paradoxification of contemporary thought-space."

Translation: *"I have no idea what I'm talking about."*

Etymological Warfare: Advanced Tactics

When someone challenges your linguistic innovations, it's time to deploy advanced defensive manoeuvres.

Defence Strategies:

1. The Historical Gambit
- Cite non-existent ancient texts
- Reference "lost" translations
- Claim alternate regional usages
- Invent medieval scholars

2. The Academic Shield
When challenged: *"Actually, in the lesser-known works of [made-up scholar], this usage was quite common among the [made-up] school of thought during the [vague historical period]."*

3. The Counter-Attack
- Question the challenger's linguistic framework
- Suggest they're using an outdated dictionary
- Claim prescriptive grammar is oppressive

- Launch into a discussion about the fluidity of language

Practical Exercises in Linguistic Confusion

1. The Coffee Shop Challenge
- Order a simple drink using at least three made-up words
- Explain the "etymology" of your invented terms
- Look disappointed when the barista doesn't understand
- Write a LinkedIn post about the experience

2. The Email Exercise

Original: *"Let's meet tomorrow to discuss the project."*

Your version: *"Vis-à-vis our impending temporal convergence, I propose a dialectical exploration of our mutual praxis-space, wherein we might synthesize our respective cognitive frameworks regarding the aforementioned paradigmatic shift in our collaborative metamorphosynthesis."*

3. The Conference Call Experiment
- Introduce three new terms per meeting
- Use them with increasing frequency
- Act surprised when others don't adopt them
- Send follow-up emails "clarifying" their meanings

Emergency Protocols for Etymology Emergencies

Sometimes you'll encounter actual linguists or classics scholars. Here's how to handle these threats to your linguistic liberty.

Emergency Responses:

1. When Caught Making Up Words
- Claim you're participating in linguistic evolution
- Declare yourself a "language artist"
- Insist you're speaking in future English
- Reference obscure dialects you just invented

2. When Faced with Real Etymology
- Dismiss it as "mainstream linguistics"
- Claim you're using pre-Indo-European roots
- Start a debate about descriptivism vs. prescriptivism
- Change the subject to Chomsky

Conclusion

Remember, dear students, the key to linguistic superiority isn't understanding language – it's using it so incorrectly that others question their own sanity. In our next chapter, we'll explore how to identify and dismiss lesser minds while maintaining an air of intellectual superiority.

Chapter 8: Field Guide to Intellectual Superiority

Identifying Lesser Minds in the Wild

Welcome back, intellectual apex predators! Now that you've mastered the art of linguistic confusion, it's time to perfect your ability to identify and properly condescend to those unfortunate souls still burdened by facts and evidence. Remember: anyone who disagrees with you is, by definition, beneath you.

Identifying Lesser Minds in the Wild

First, we must learn to spot those who haven't achieved our level of enlightened ignorance. Like any good naturalist, we'll create a taxonomy of intellectual inferiors.

Classification of Lesser Minds:

1. The Fact-Checker (Verificatus annoying)
- Natural Habitat: Comment sections, academic institutions
- Identifying Marks: Carries source materials, uses citations
- Call: "Actually, according to the data..."
- Defence Strategy: Declare data a social construct

A Satire on Intellectual Pretension

2. The Expert (Knowledgeous threatensis)

Field Notes:

- Dangerous species known to use peer-reviewed research
- Often has relevant degrees and actual experience
- May attempt to correct your magnificent wrongness
- Must be avoided or shouted down immediately

3. The Critical Thinker (Logicus inconvenientus)

- Distinguished by ability to spot logical fallacies
- Dangerous tendency to ask for evidence
- Known to question circular reasoning
- Must be buried in word salad until retreats

*4. The Practical Person
(Commonsensus vulgaris)*
- Relies on "real-world experience"
- Dismisses theoretical frameworks
- Asks "But does it work?"
- Counter with increasingly abstract terminology

The Art of the Dismissive Hand Wave

The dismissive hand wave is your physical manifestation of intellectual superiority. When properly executed, it can dismiss decades of research with a single gesture.

Hand Wave Techniques:

1. Basic Movements
- The "That's Just Your Opinion" Flick

A Satire on Intellectual Pretension

- The "I'm Above This" Flutter
- The "You Wouldn't Understand" Sweep
- The "I Can't Even" Flourish

2. Advanced Gestures

Situation: *Someone presents evidence*

Response: *Combine wrist rotation with eye roll*

Effect: *Suggests their peer-reviewed study is beneath contempt*

Follow-up: *Mutter something about paradigm shifts*

3. Master Level Movements

- The "I've Transcended Facts" Float
- The "Your Evidence Is Boring Me" Swish
- The "I'm Having a Thought" Temple Tap
- The "You're Not Worth My Time" Backhand

When to Say "Well, Actually..."

Timing is everything when deploying your favourite phrase. Like a linguistic ninja, you must strike when your target least expects it.

Optimal "Well, Actually..." Moments:

1. Prime Opportunities
- During emotional personal stories
- Mid-sentence in someone else's presentation
- At funerals (especially regarding the deceased's grammar)
- When someone expresses joy about anything

2. Advanced Interruption Timing

Speaker: *"My grandmother just—"*

You: *"Well, actually, the term 'grandmother' is problematically heteronormative in its genealogical assumptions..."*

3. Expert Level Deployments
- During wedding vows
- In the middle of jokes
- While someone is giving birth
- During moments of national crisis

Field Research Techniques

To maintain superiority, you must study your intellectual inferiors in their natural habitats.

Observation Guidelines:

1. Research Locations
- Coffee shops (observe the uncultured ordering drip coffee)
- Bookstores (watch people buying bestsellers instead of obscure philosophy)
- Universities (but only to critique them)
- Social media (your natural habitat)

2. Documentation Methods

Field Notes Format:

Date: *[Current date]*

Subject: *[Lesser mind engaging in learning]*

Observation: *[Their pathetic attempt to understand]*

Your Intervention: *[How you corrected them unnecessarily]*

3. Classification System
- Level 1: Still believes in objective truth
- Level 2: Cites sources
- Level 3: Admits to not knowing everything
- Level 4: Values practical experience
- Level 5: Actually listens to others (most concerning)

Emergency Protocols for Intellectual Threats

Sometimes you'll encounter someone who threatens your intellectual superiority. Here's how to handle these situations.

Threat Response Procedures:
1. When Faced with Actual Expertise
- Question the entire field of study
- Invoke conspiracy theories

- Create a new field of study where you're the expert
- Change the subject to consciousness

2. When Confronted with Facts

Step 1: Dismiss source as biased

Step 2: Question methodology

Step 3: Invoke quantum physics

Step 4: If all else fails, claim to be conducting a social experiment

3. When Logic Is Used Against You

- Declare logic a Western construct
- Appeal to higher consciousness
- Create your own system of logic
- Start speaking in koans

A Satire on Intellectual Pretension

Practical Exercises in Superiority

1. The Coffee Shop Experiment
- Correct everyone's orders
- Explain why their coffee preferences are philosophically flawed
- Write a thread about how no one understands true coffee
- Look disappointed when anyone enjoys their drink

2. The Bookstore Challenge
- Reorganize self-help books into "beneath contempt" section
- Leave notes in bestsellers about their obvious flaws
- Loudly sigh when people buy popular books
- Give unsolicited lectures in the philosophy section

3. The Social Media Safari
- Find happy people
- Explain why their joy is theoretically unsound
- Create threads about the problems with their worldview
- Block anyone who agrees with them

Conclusion

Remember, dear intellectual warriors, maintaining superiority isn't just about being condescending – it's about being condescending with style. Your dismissiveness should be so refined that others question not just their knowledge, but their entire reality.

Appendix A: Common Phrases for the Modern Know-It-All

Essential Vocabulary for the Professional Pseudo-Intellectual

Introduction: The Power of Pretentious Phrasing

Welcome to your ultimate phrasebook of intellectual superiority! In this appendix, we'll explore the essential expressions that every aspiring know-it-all must master. Remember: it's not what you say, but how condescendingly you say it.

Section 1: "I don't mean to be pedantic, but..." (And Other Lies)

Let's begin with the crown jewel of intellectual posturing: phrases that pretend to apologize for exactly what you're trying to do.

Core Phrases and Their True Meanings:

1. The Classic Openings

What You Say: *"I don't mean to be pedantic, but..."*

What You Mean: *"I absolutely live to be pedantic, and here comes my moment"*

What You Say: *"Not to play devil's advocate, but..."*

A Satire on Intellectual Pretension

What You Mean: *"I'm about to defend an indefensible position for attention"*

What You Say: *"With all due respect..."*

What You Mean: *"I'm showing precisely zero respect"*

2. Advanced Qualifiers
- "In point of fact..."
- "If you think about it critically..."
- "From a purely objective standpoint..."
- "In the grand scheme of things..."
- "Philosophically speaking..."

3. Emergency Backpedalling
- "I'm just engaging in Socratic dialogue"
- "I'm merely fostering intellectual discourse"
- "I'm simply encouraging critical thinking"

- "I'm playing devil's advocate for the sake of discussion"

Section 2: "As Someone Who..."

The art of establishing unearned authority through vague credentials and tangential experiences.

Authority-Building Templates:

1. Academic Posturing
- "As someone who's studied [subject you read one article about]..."
- "Having spent considerable time thinking about..."
- "In my extensive research..." (Googled it once)
- "Drawing from my background in..." (Watched a YouTube video)

2. Experience Claims
- "As someone who once dated a physicist..."
- "Having lived near a university..."
- "Given my experience with reading books..."
- "As a person who owns a telescope..."

3. Intellectual Heritage
- "As an individual who's deeply immersed in..."
- "Speaking as someone who's wrestled with these concepts..."
- "From my vantage point as a free-thinking intellectual..."

Section 3: "In My Expert Opinion..."

The fine art of declaring expertise without any actual qualifications.

Expert Opinion Formulations:

1. Basic Declarations
- "In my considered opinion..."
- "From my analytical perspective..."
- "Based on my comprehensive understanding..."
- "Drawing from my synthesis of the literature..."

2. Advanced Authority Claims
- "My research suggests..." (Read a Wikipedia article)
- "Studies I'm familiar with indicate..." (Saw a tweet about it)
- "The data clearly shows..." (Looking at one cherry-picked statistic)
- "Historical precedent demonstrates..." (Watched a History Channel show)

3. Emergency Expertise

When challenged: *"I've been studying this independently for years"*

When pressed for credentials: *"I prefer to let my ideas stand on their merit"*

When asked for sources: *"I synthesize multiple perspectives"*

Section 4: Transitional Phrases for Intellectual Combat

Essential phrases for when you need to change the subject or avoid admitting ignorance.

Strategic Transitions:

1. Topic Avoidance
- "That's an interesting point, but let's examine the meta-issue..."

- "While that's relevant on a surface level..."
- "Your perspective is valid, however..." (It's not valid)
- "Let's take a step back and consider..."

2. Emergency Exits
- "This reminds me of a more fundamental question..."
- "Perhaps we should interrogate our assumptions..."
- "The real issue here is..."
- "Let's problematize this narrative..."

3. Intellectual Escape Hatches

When cornered: *"We're approaching this from different paradigms"*

When proven wrong: *"That's a rather reductive view"*

When confused: *"Let's deconstruct this further"*

A Satire on Intellectual Pretension

Section 5: Power Phrases for Social Media

Specially crafted phrases for maximum impact in the digital sphere.

Digital Dominance Expressions:

1. Thread Starters
- "Unpopular opinion, but..."
- "Let's talk about what no one is discussing..."
- "A thread on why everything you know about [topic] is wrong:"
- "Prepare to have your mind blown..."

2. Engagement Bait
- "I said what I said."
- "This might be too complex for some, but..."

- "Not everyone is ready for this conversation"
- "Let that sink in."

3. Mic Drop Moments
- "But you're not ready for that discussion"
- "I'll wait while you process that"
- "Think about it"
- "Do better"

Conclusion: The Power of Phrases

Remember, these phrases are your armour in the battle against actual knowledge and expertise. Use them wisely, use them often, and never, ever admit you might be wrong.

Appendix B: Certificates of Expertise

Print-Your-Own Credentials and Other Intellectual Status Symbols

Welcome to the final frontier of intellectual posturing: the creation and maintenance of entirely fictional credentials. Remember, in a world where actual experts have spent years studying their fields, you have something better: the ability to make things up with absolute confidence.

Print-Your-Own Credentials

The art of creating impressive-sounding credentials that mean absolutely nothing.

Credential Creation Guide:

1. Title Generation

Basic Formula: *[Impressive Word] + [Academic-Sounding Field] + [Important Title]*

Examples:
- Distinguished Fellow of Meta-Cognitive Studies
- Chief Theoretical Officer of Post-Modern Thought
- Advanced Practitioner of Quantum Consciousness
- Master of Trans-Dimensional Philosophy

2. Institution Invention

Template: *The [Famous Location] Institute of [Made-Up Field]*

Sample Institutions:

- The Cambridge-Adjacent Institute of Theoretical Everything
- The Almost-Oxford Academy of Advanced Thinking
- The Vaguely European University of Meta Studies
- The International Society of Self-Certified Geniuses

3. Certification Design

- Use lots of gold foil (or just yellow highlighter)
- Add random Latin phrases
- Include at least three official-looking seals
- Mandatory calligraphy font
- Bonus: Coffee stain for authenticity

How to Create a Wikipedia Page About Yourself

Because if it's on Wikipedia, it must be true (until they delete it for "lack of notability").

Wikipedia Presence Strategy:

1. Page Creation Basics
Essential Elements:

- Born: [Date] (be vague if possible)
- Notable for: "Contributions to [field you just made up]"
- Known for: "Challenging conventional wisdom about [basic concept]"
- Influences: List of philosophers you haven't read

2. Career Section Enhancement
- List speaking engagements at your local coffee shop

- Include papers published on your blog
- Reference your YouTube channel as "digital symposiums"
- Cite your tweets as "published works"

3. Controversy Section Management

How to Handle Deletions:

- Claim censorship by the intellectual establishment
- Create multiple sock puppet accounts
- Write blog posts about Wikipedia's bias
- Start a petition to "protect alternative knowledge"

Template for Your TED Talk Application

Because nothing says "intellectual" like standing on a red carpet circle.

TED Talk Essential Elements:

1. Compelling Titles

Formula: *"How [Basic Concept] Is Actually [Unrelated Complex Topic]"*

Examples:

- "How My Morning Coffee Revealed the Nature of Consciousness"
- "Why Everything You Know About Everything Is Wrong"
- "The Quantum Physics of Making Toast"
- "What My Cat Taught Me About Post-Structural Economics"

2. Talk Structure
- Start with a personal anecdote that definitely didn't happen
- Include at least one misinterpreted scientific study

- Show incomprehensible graphs
- End with a call to action that means nothing

3. Stage Presence Tips

Essential Movements:

- The Thoughtful Pace
- The Meaningful Pause
- The "This Will Blow Your Mind" Gesture
- The "I Just Said Something Profound" Nod

Creating Your Academic-Looking Website

Because .edu domains are overrated anyway.

Website Essential Elements:

1. Domain Name Selection

Formula: *[Your Name] + [Intellectual Term].com*

Examples:

- YourNameThinks.com
- YourNameParadigm.com
- YourNameTheory.com
- MetaCognitiveYourName.com

2. Required Pages

- "About" (minimum 5,000 words about your journey to enlightenment)
- "Publications" (links to your Medium articles)
- "Speaking" (that time you gave a presentation in high school)
- "Contact" (for serious intellectual inquiries only)

3. Visual Elements
Must-Have Features:

- Black and white photo of you looking contemplative
- Quote from yourself in italics
- Library background
- Unnecessarily complex navigation menu

Emergency Credential Defence Protocols

For when someone questions your expertise.

Defence Strategies:

1. When Challenged About Credentials
Standard Responses:

- "I prefer to let my ideas speak for themselves"

- "Traditional credentials are a construct of the establishment"
- "Einstein was a patent clerk"
- "My work transcends conventional academic boundaries"

2. Documentation Demands

- Claim your certificates were lost in a very specific fire
- Mention your upcoming book deal (perpetually upcoming)
- Reference private studies you can't share
- Pivot to questioning their credentials

3. Ultimate Fallbacks

Last Resort Phrases:

- "I'm actually conducting a study on credential privilege"
- "My work is too cutting-edge for traditional certification"
- "I've moved beyond the need for institutional validation"

- "Would you ask Socrates for his diploma?"

Conclusion: The Art of Credential Creation

Remember, dear students of intellectual posturing, credentials are just pieces of paper – which is exactly why you should create your own. In a world obsessed with "proof" and "verification," be the change you wish to see: completely unverifiable.

Index of Obscure References to Drop in Conversation

(Arranged by pretentiousness level)

Level 1: Amateur Hour

- Schrödinger's Cat (Entry level - use only if desperate)
- Occam's Razor (Pronounce it wrong for extra authenticity)
- Plato's Cave (Best paired with "we're all just living in...")
- The Butterfly Effect (Bonus points for mentioning the movie)

Level 2: Intermediate Pretension

- Hegelian Dialectic (No need to understand it, just mention "thesis-antithesis-synthesis")

A Satire on Intellectual Pretension

- Cartesian Dualism (Just say "I think, therefore I am" in French)
- Kafkaesque (Can be applied to any mildly inconvenient situation)
- Zeitgeist (Must be whispered dramatically)
- Paradigm Shift (Use whenever anything changes, no matter how minor)

Level 3: Professional Pomposity

- The Categorical Imperative (Never explain which one)
- Foucault's Panopticon (Excellent for criticizing office layout)
- Sisyphean (Use to describe any repetitive task, especially doing dishes)
- Weltanschauung (German words automatically add 50 pretension points)
- Post-post-ironic (Nobody knows what this means, which is perfect)

Level 4: Galaxy Brain

- Phenomenological epistemology (Just nod sagely after saying it)
- Linguistic relativism (Best used when correcting someone's grammar)
- The Sapir-Whorf Hypothesis (Mention after watching any foreign film)
- Ontological determinism (Excellent excuse for being late to meetings)
- Hermeneutic circle (Use when you're going in circles in an argument)

Level 5: Ultimate Enlightenment

- Baudrillard's simulacra (Must be referenced when discussing any reality TV)
- The Lacanian Real (Particularly effective when complaining about coffee)
- Derridean différance (The silent 'a' is crucial - point this out repeatedly)

- Žižek's critique of ideology *sniff* (The sniff is mandatory)
- Quantum superposition (Can be applied to literally anything non-quantum)

Emergency Backup References

- "As Wittgenstein would say..." (Follow with literally anything)
- "This reminds me of Camus' thoughts on..." (Trail off meaningfully)
- "Through the lens of critical theory..." (No need to specify which one)
- "The Japanese have a word for this..." (Make one up confidently)
- "In the original Greek..." (No one will check)

Situational Applications

For Dating Apps:
- "Seeking a dialectical relationship"
- "Looking for someone to share existential dread with"
- "Must understand post-structural memes"

For Work Meetings:
- "This project has become rather Sisyphean"
- "Let's examine this through a post-modern lens"
- "The metrics are merely a social construct"

For Social Media:
- #NoumenalRealm
- #CartesianAnxiety
- #HegelianMoment
- #CategorialImperativeButInAFunWay

Warning Labels

- "Use with caution in academic settings"
- "May cause severe eye-rolling in educated company"
- "Side effects may include social isolation and uninvited lectures"
- "Best served with a smug expression and a turtleneck sweater"

Note: *This index should be memorized and deployed strategically for maximum impact. Remember, it's not about understanding these references - it's about using them with unshakeable confidence. As Aristotle probably said, "Fake it till you make it."*

For advanced studies, please see our companion volume: "Making Up Quotes: Attribution as a Social Construct"

Copyright

Copyright © 2025 by Mwape Kalembwe. All rights reserved under international copyright laws. Upon payment of the necessary fees, you are granted a nonexclusive, non-transferable right to view and read this e-book on-screen. Reproduction, transmission, downloading, decompiling, reverse-engineering, or storage of any part of this text in any format or by any means, whether electronic or mechanical, is prohibited without the express written consent of Such Academy books.

Printed in Dunstable, United Kingdom

66204697R00077